The Sword of the Viking King

TERRY DEARY'S
VIKING TALES

The Sword of the Viking King

Illustrated by Helen Flook

A & C Black • London

First published 2010 by
A & C Black
an imprint of Bloomsbury Publishing Plc
50 Bedford Square, London, WC1B 3DP

www.bloomsbury.com

Text copyright © 2010 Terry Deary
Illustrations copyright © 2010 Helen Flook

The rights of Terry Deary and Helen Flook to be identified as the
author and illustrator of this work have been asserted by them in
accordance with the Copyrights, Designs and Patents Act 1988.

ISBN 978-1-4081-2237-2

A CIP catalogue for this book is available from the British Library.

This book is produced using paper that is made from wood grown in
managed, sustainable forests. It is natural, renewable and recyclable.
The logging and manufacturing processes conform to the
environmental regulations of the country of origin.

Printed and Bound by CPI Group (UK) Ltd, Croydon CR0 4YY

3 5 7 9 10 8 6 4 2

Chapter One
The Soldier

Wessex, England, 878

"Call yourself a soldier?" the boy said. He stood in the doorway of a poor cottage made of wood and mud. He crossed his arms and looked at the man who stood outside on the dusty path that led into the woods.

The man wore armour made of leather and a helmet of iron. His face was a mask of blood and dust. "Well, I've fought a dozen battles, so I suppose that makes me a soldier," he said. "What is your name?"

"Ethelbert," the boy said.

"Ah, I had a brother called Ethelbert," the soldier sighed. "He died. He was killed at the Battle of Merton."

"I'm sorry," Ethelbert said. "But you're still not much of a soldier, are you?"

"I do my best," the man sighed again.

"I'm sure you do," Ethelbert said. "What I'm saying is this ... the Vikings keep beating us English. They beat us over in the east and now they're heading this way."

"We did win a few battles," the soldier offered.

"You haven't *stopped* them though, have you?" Ethelbert said, his small face turning red with rage. "They will take over Wessex and that will be *it*, my mum says. The Vikings will rule the whole of England. English children like me will be killed or become Viking slaves. And *you* ... you soldiers ... you are useless."

The soldier leaned wearily against the wall of the cottage. "I know we lost the last battle, but next time..."

"*Next* time, King Gudrun the Viking will *smash* you, and his army will burn down our house. That's what my mum says," Ethelbert told the soldier.

"Your mum says a lot," the soldier said.

"They call her Gytha the Grim because she's so tough. My mum says that King Alfred is as much use as a bucket with a hole in it. Do you know, he *paid* the Vikings to go away?"

"Yes..."

"My mum says *she* could fight better than King Alfred. And my mum is never wrong. My mum reckons *I* could fight better than him. If I was a couple of years older, I'd beat King Gudrun with one hand tied behind my back."

The soldier blew out his cheeks. Dust from his lips speckled the sunlight that shone through the trees. "Do you think you could let me have a drink ... a little ale? A bit of bread and cheese? Our army is scattered. I need to get back to our fort at Athelney."

"Don't let me stop you," Ethelbert said with a sneer. "Better hurry or the Vikings might catch you."

"Would your mother be able to give me a little food?" the soldier said.

Ethelbert sighed loudly, as if it was too much trouble to ask. But he looked through the low doorway and called, "Mum! There's a man here who wants some food!"

"We don't feed beggars," came the reply from inside. "Anyway, I'm busy baking."

The soldier leaned in and said, "I'm a soldier, madam. I'm not a beggar."

The woman had a pinched, mean-mouthed face like her son. She looked up from the fire where small, flat loaves were baking on an iron pan.

"If you want some bread, you can earn it, young man," she snapped. "You can watch the pan while me and young Bert gather more wood."

The soldier lifted his sack of weapons through the door, took off his helmet and sank onto a chair by the fire. "Thank you," he said with a tired smile. "You will be rewarded."

The woman looked at his weapon sack. "A soldier, eh?"

"Yes, madam."

"You're not much good, are you?"

The man shook his head. "Ethelbert has already told me that."

Chapter Two
Gytha the Grim

"Now," Gytha said. "The loaves are toasting nicely, see?" She spoke to the soldier as if he were a child.

"Yes, madam."

"Now, when they are nice and brown, you take a flat knife ... see it here on the table? The flat knife?"

"Yes, madam."

"And you use the knife to turn the loaves over to let them bake on the other side. But if you *don't* turn them over, they will get burned on the bottom, and I will be very cross. Do I make myself clear?"

"You don't want to make Gytha the Grim cross," Ethelbert said with a chuckle. "Dad upset her yesterday and he got a slap with that cooking pot. You should have heard the crack! Oooof!"

"I'll be careful," the soldier promised.

"There's ale in that jug on the table. Help yourself. You can have one of the loaves when they've finished cooking."

Gytha grabbed her son by the arm and dragged him outside. "Come on, Bert. Let's get some more wood before that fire dies."

The soldier opened his sack. He pulled out his sword and looked at the edge in the light of the fire. It was blunt and chipped and stained with Viking blood. He took out a stone and began to rub it along the blade until it was sharp again. Then he took out the arrows he had gathered as he ran from the battlefield. Some needed to have their tips sharpened, too.

The soldier sat, slumped and unhappy. He wondered if he'd ever have a chance to use those arrows, or if the Vikings would attack before the English army could gather themselves together.

The smoke from the fire stung his eyes and soon the smell of burning wood was mixed with the smell of burning bread.

"No-o!" the soldier wailed, as he snatched at the hot pan. It burned his hand as he pulled it away from the fire, and he dropped it in the hearth. The loaves tumbled into the cold ashes.

The man snatched them up, blew off the ash and tried to use his knife to scrape away the burned crust. He had just replaced the last one when the door opened and the woman marched in.

Gytha picked up a cooking pot and walked towards the soldier. "You clown. You useless lump of cattle dung. I gave you one simple job. Look after the loaves. Nothing else. But could you do it? Could you?"

"Hit him, Ma!" Ethelbert giggled. "Hit him with the pot like you did to Dad!"

"Wait!" the soldier cried, jumping to his feet. "I will pay for the damage. As soon as I get to Athelney, I'll send money."

The woman held the pot, ready to swing it. "You will leave here and I'll never see you again. I'm not stupid."

"I'll leave something with you then ... something valuable," the man promised.

"Such as?" the woman asked.

"Just hit him, Ma!" Ethelbert crowed.

The soldier plunged a hand into his sack and pulled out a wide band of gold. It glowed in the light of the fire.

"What is it?" the woman breathed.

"It's my crown. The crown of England," the man said quickly.

"*Your* crown?" Ethelbert said. "You mean a crown you stole from the king?"

"No," the man said. "I *am* the king. I am King Alfred and this is my crown."

Ethelbert's mouth went dry. "Better not hit him, Ma."

Chapter Three
King Alfred

"Your holiness!" the woman croaked.
"Your heavenliness! King Alfred himself?
Well I never ... ooooh ... I
don't know what to say."

"You could tell him what you think of him," young Ethelbert said.

"I think he's a hero," the woman said quickly.

"No, Ma, you said he was as much use as a bucket with a hole in it," the boy reminded her.

The woman ground her teeth tight and spoke through them. "No, I didn't, Bert. I was talking about your *father*."

"You said *you* could do a better job than King Alfred. You said the village mole catcher could do a better job than King Alfred. You said..."

"All *right*, Bert," the woman hissed. "I know what you *think* I said. But I didn't. You are losing your memory. They say you can cure that with a sharp blow to the head ... with something like a cooking pot."

Ethelbert went pale. "I remember now, Ma. You said King Alfred is a hero."

The woman gave a sharp nod, then turned back to the king. "Sorry I shouted at you. If I'd *known*..."

"No, Gytha, you were right," said King Alfred. "I was careless. I have so much in my head at the moment."

"You nearly had a cooking pot in your head," the boy said with a grin.

His mother glared at him. "I didn't expect to see a king wandering through a farming village like ours," Gytha explained. "And all alone."

"I had a boy – a squire. He carried my weapons, looked after my horse. The Vikings captured him," King Alfred said. "Now I need to find my way back to Athelney and meet up with my army. I thought I was on the road to Glastonbury, but I got hopelessly lost."

"Lots of people do, your worship,"
Gytha said with a sigh. "But my son,
Ethelbert, knows the roads around here
like a cattle drover. He helps his father
take the cows to all the markets. You could
show him the way to Athelney, couldn't
you, Bert?"

"I could take him all the way," the boy
said. "I could even go to the next battle
with him."

"You're too young to fight, my little
lamb," the woman gasped.

"*You* said I could fight better than King Alfred. If I was a couple of years older, *you* said I'd beat King Gudrun with one hand tied behind my back."

"I never said that," the woman shouted. "Anyway, you're not a couple of years older, and you're not a soldier."

"No, but I could carry the king's weapons, and hold his horse while he goes into battle ... be a *squire*," Ethelbert said.

The woman put down the pot on the table and picked up the crown. "What do you think, your grace?"

"I think I need all the help I can get. I'd be glad to take your son with me," King Alfred said.

"That's settled, then," Gytha said. "I'll pack him a few clothes."

"And some food for the journey," King Alfred reminded her.

The woman nodded. "I have some lovely cheese," she said. "And the bread is fresh ... it's just a little bit burned. I hope you don't mind?"

King Alfred laughed. "Blame the kitchen boy who was left to watch the loaves."

Chapter Four
The Road to Athelney

Ethelbert led King Alfred along the path through the woods. They reached a larger road, where they met a group of weary English soldiers who were heading for the fort at Athelney.

The king joined the soldiers and tried to cheer them up. "We were just unlucky," he said. "Next time we'll win."

"We have no choice," a soldier told him. "We must fight or the Vikings will crush us like corn in a millstone."

Ethelbert asked, "Where will we fight them next, sir?"

The king shook his head. "I don't know. I don't want to sit and wait for them to march on Athelney."

"Is that what they're planning to do?" the boy asked.

Alfred shrugged. "I don't know what they're planning. I wish I did. I want to attack them when they aren't expecting it."

Ethelbert walked on in silence for a while, then he said, "I suppose you could find out their plan."

"Walk into their camp? Go up to Gudrun and ask him what he's going to do next?" the king said with a bitter smile.

"Something like that," Ethelbert said. "Dad and I go poaching deer in the woods."

"You're a poacher?"

Ethelbert shrugged. "I'm a thief. It's my job. And I never get caught. It's a tough job, but somebody has to do it."

"No, they don't," King Alfred argued. "Anyway, I don't understand what going poaching has to do with slipping into Gudrun's camp."

"Father and I take the skin and the head of a dead deer. We dress ourselves up in it, then we creep up to the herd. We look like a deer, we smell like a deer. And the rest of the deer don't know we're there."

"Ethelred, you're brilliant!" said King Alfred.

"I know. That's what Mum's always saying."

"I dress up as a Viking and I walk into the Viking camp. I can speak Danish," the king went on, excited at the idea.

"Do you have Viking weapons and armour?" the boy asked.

"No, I don't," Alfred admitted.

"So you can't enter as a warrior. You'll have to go in as something else," Ethelbert said.

King Alfred clicked his fingers. "The Vikings love hearing poems about their heroes. If I went in as a minstrel, I could get really close to Gudrun."

"You'll need a servant to lead your horse," Ethelbert said.

"Who do you think could do that?"

The boy stopped. "Me, of course. It was my idea, after all."

King Alfred frowned and looked down at the boy. "If it goes wrong ... if they find out who I really am ... they'll kill me. And they'll kill you, too, Ethelbert."

"Ha! They can try," the boy said. "If they harm one hair on my head they'll be sorry. Gytha the Grim will get Gudrun. She'll use his skull to drink her ale. Don't you worry about that."

King Alfred smiled. "And if they burn her bread, she'll wipe out the whole Viking army."

"She will," said Ethelbert. "So shall we do it?"

King Alfred nodded. "We shall."

Chapter Five
The Sword

King Gudrun of the Vikings was in a good mood. He walked around the camp and talked to his warriors. "One more battle, lads. One more and the English will be finished."

"About time," an old soldier with purple scars and a battered helmet said. "I'm ready to settle down. I want to bring my family here and be a farmer."

"You'll have the best farm in the land, Eric," his king promised.

"If we win," the man grumbled.

King Gudrun pulled a sword from his belt. "The sword of Freyr," he said.

"Freyr is the god of peace," Eric reminded him.

"Yes! Peace. That is what we'll bring to England, even if we have to kill every last Englishman. A country full of dead, Eric, you don't get much more peaceful than that."

The old warrior laughed. "Can I keep a few alive to work as slaves?"

"You can keep all the ones you capture in the next battle," Gudrun said.

"Where will that be?" the soldier asked.

"There's a meeting of all the captains in my tent tonight. We'll decide then. Not that it matters. With the sword of Freyr, we will win. It's my lucky sword."

"It didn't help us at the Battle of Ashdown," Eric said.

"That's what I'm saying. I wasn't at the Battle of Ashdown with the sword of Freyr, was I? And the Vikings lost. But I *am* here now. This time we can't lose."

"I'm pleased to hear it," a man said.

King Gudrun swung round to see who had spoken. A tall man was standing there with a pack on his back. Beside him stood a sharp-eyed boy.

"Who are you?" the king snapped.

"A minstrel, sir," the stranger said. "I travel from camp to camp and tell my stories."

"English camps?" the king asked. "Do you go to English camps?"

"Not any longer," the minstrel said. "They are too miserable and beaten. They just want to go home and hide."

"But they still have a camp, don't they?"

"They are camped near Ethandun. If you attack them there, they will melt like butter in the sun."

"Ethandun, eh? Then that's what I'll tell the captains tonight," Gudrun said with a tight smile. "King Alfred won't be expecting that."

The minstrel looked at the boy and whispered, "Or maybe King Alfred *will* be expecting it, eh, Ethelbert?"

The boy grinned. "I'm sure you will, King Alfred. Ha ha!"

Chapter Six
The Minstrel

That night, the Viking captains feasted on the English cattle and sheep they had stolen. They drank stolen mead and ale and met in King Gudrun's tent. They were a happy band.

"My brothers," the king roared over the noise. He waited till the men went quiet. Today we feast..."

Cheers.

"Tomorrow we rest..."

More cheers.

"And the next day we march to Ethandun. The English are there. I know they are there. But they don't know that I know they're there. Now *you* know they're there ... but they don't know that you know that I know they're there. We will take them by surprise and crush them."

Loudest cheers of all.

Gudrun held up his sword. "By the sword of Freyr herself, I swear we will not lose. This is our lucky charm. With Freyr's luck and blessing we can conquer the world."

Happy laughter.

"Now, while you eat and drink, we have a minstrel here to tell you a tale of heroes. Viking heroes. One day, minstrels will sing about *you* and your great victory at Ethandun." He turned to Alfred. "So, minstrel, what tale do you have for us tonight?"

Alfred stepped forward. "Why, the tale of Freyr and his sword, of course."

"Of course," the Viking king nodded, and sat at the table with his warrior chiefs.

Alfred waited till the men were quiet ... quiet except for the noises of men eating, slurping and belching, and of dogs crunching on bones, or yelping as they chased rats from the tent.

At last he began.

Alfred told the tale of Freyr and the sword that fought all by itself. No one could defeat him while he owned the sword.

"Great Freyr, the god, he fell in love,
With lovely Gerda, what a dove.
'Please marry me? I have to know.'
But Gerda said, 'The answer's no.'"

Freyr was upset, Alfred said, but his servant assured him that he'd win Gerda's heart for his master. And Freyr promised the servant his magic sword, if he managed it.

"The servant said to Gerda fair,
'There's no one finer than my Freyr.
Just marry him, his heart is true.'
She changed her mind and said, 'I do.'"

The poem was a very long one. The Viking warriors cheered when Freyr won Gerda. But most had fallen asleep by the time Alfred reached the last part of the poem.

The story moved onto the great battle at the end of the world. Gods against giants. When the gods fight in that battle, who will be the first to die? Freyr, of course. He'd given away his magic sword.

"Freyr fought, the foolish lord.
And lost without his magic sword."

By then, all the Vikings were snoring. King Alfred smiled at young Ethelbert. "Are we ready to go?" he asked.

"Oh, yes," the boy nodded. "We're ready."

Chapter Seven
The Battle

King Alfred stood on Ethandun hill and watched as the Viking army marched its dusty way towards him.

"Are they mad?" his general, Athelstan, asked. "Do they want to be beaten?"

"They think they *can't* be beaten," Ethelbert said.

"We have a great army. Half of England's finest warriors have come to King Alfred's side," Athelstan said. "We are on top of a hill. We will shoot them down with arrows as they climb. If any reach the top, with their heavy leather armour and great iron swords, they'll be too tired to fight."

The Viking army lined up at the bottom of the hill. They left their carts with tents and food on the road and made ready to charge.

"Which madman decided Ethandun Hill was the best place to fight?"

"I was the madman," King Alfred said, and he laughed. "But Gudrun is maddest of all ... he took the word of a travelling minstrel."

The English king turned to his army. He raised the sword of Freyr above his head. "We cannot lose. We have the hilltop ... and we have a lucky charm. For England ... and for freedom!" he cried.

"For freedom!" his soldiers cried and turned to face the scrambling, slipping sweating, staggering, sliding Viking soldiers.

The first rows of Vikings fell under a black rain of arrows. The next row had to climb over their moaning, bleeding friends. Only the strongest reached the top and raised their weary arms with swords that felt as heavy as lead.

Gudrun and Eric were the first to reach the top. The king turned and called back to his straining men, "Come on! Let's finish them off. Eric, fetch me the sword of Freyr."

"I don't have it," Eric muttered quietly. "I thought you had it."

"*I* don't have it," the Viking king hissed. "I thought *you* did."

"You've lost it," Eric said.

"So find it," the king said under his breath.

"It's a bit late to start looking now," Eric groaned. "We're facing a thousand Englishmen who want our blood.

Gudrun sighed. "Don't let them see you're scared," he told his captain.

"I'm not," Eric replied.

The Viking king looked at the line of English soldiers. They stood shoulder to shoulder. "Come on," he panted and raised a common iron sword. "Who will be the first to die?"

The English soldiers didn't move.

Eric rested on his sword a moment. "Why not send out your leader, the young Alfred. Let him fight me, man to man. If I beat him, then you surrender – I'll let you live to be my slaves."

King Alfred stepped forward from the line of soldiers. "And if you lose?"

"I know your face," the Viking king said. "I've met you somewhere, haven't I?"

Alfred nodded.

"*Great Freyr, the god, he fell in love, With lovely Gerda, what a dove,*" he said.

"The minstrel? A spy? A coward's trick," the Viking king sneered.

"I asked what will happen when you lose?" Alfred said.

"I won't lose," Gudrun said.

Alfred looked over his shoulder. "Ethelbert?" he called. "Come here. Show King Gudrun what a wicked English thief took before we left his camp."

Ethelbert stood alongside his king. He held out the sword of Freyr.

"*Gudrun fought, the foolish lord. He lost without his magic sword*," Alfred said.

"My sword!" Gudrun cried. "My lucky sword. I cannot fight without it."

"What shall we do with your body, Gudrun?" King Alfred said. "Bury it here or send it back to Denmark?"

Gudrun threw down the old iron sword he had been carrying. "Alfred, my friend," he said. "I'm glad we've met this way. I wanted to talk to you about peace."

Alfred nodded. He placed an arm around the shoulder of young Ethelbert. "Peace? Yes. I don't want boys like Ethelbert here to grow up fighting and dying. Peace would be good."

Ethelbert clutched the sword and watched as King Alfred walked across the grassy hilltop to shake the Viking king by the hand. The boy was sure he felt the sword of Freyr glowing warm in his hand. He looked at it.

"Peace? Yes, Freyr, you would like that," he smiled.

Epilogue

There is a famous story of King Alfred burning the loaves in a peasant woman's cottage. She gave him a telling off before she found out who he was. We don't know if the story is true.

There is another story that says he went into the Viking camp, disguised as a minstrel, and learned their plans.

In the last great battle, Alfred beat Gudrun and the Vikings at Ethandun Hill. Gudrun gave up and Alfred let him live. The English and the Vikings divided the country between them. They lived in peace while Alfred ruled.

The Viking god Freyr gave his name to a day of the week ... Freyr-day ... or Friday as we call it. The story of him giving up his magical sword for the love of Gerda is one of the old Viking stories they liked to tell.

We don't know what day the battle of Ethandun was fought. It would be nice to think it was fought on Freyr-day, wouldn't it?

TERRY DEARY'S KNIGHTS' TALES